Special Message

_____

_____

_____

_____

_____

_____

With Love, _____

Stick your favorite
picture here

Hannah

is surrounded with so much love.
You may even think it comes from above.

Hannah

You are loved by the sky and the sun.

You deserve happiness and to have so much fun.

Hannah

You are loved by the trees and the leaves that fall.
You are loved by everyone and all.

Hannah

You are loved by the wind and the breeze.
You deserve the best hugging squeeze.

Hannah

You are loved by the birds that tweet.
All because you are so gentle and sweet.

Hannah

You are loved by the flowers
in the ground.
There is so much love all around.

Hannah

You are loved by the moon and night.
You shine like the stars with the brightest light.

Hannah

You are loved with your beautiful heart.

You are beautiful, amazing, and oh so smart.

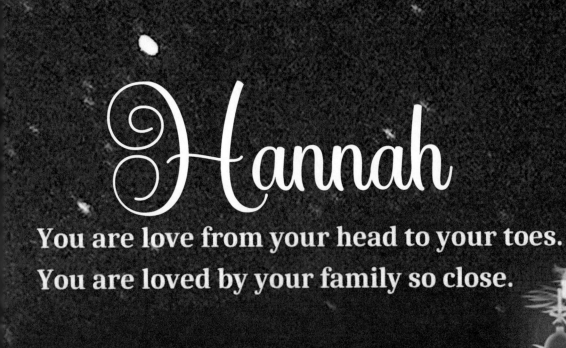

Hannah

You are love from your head to your toes.

You are loved by your family so close.

Merry Christmas.
Love, Grandma

Hannah

You will be loved for the rest of your days.
You will be loved forever and always.

The end